The Drive

Helen Oxenbury

WALKER BOOKS

AND SUBSIDIARIES

LONDON • BOSTON • SYDNEY

One day we went for a drive.
Mum made some sandwiches.

For Jan

First published 1983 by Walker Books Ltd
87 Vauxhall Walk, London SE11 5HJ

This edition published 2001

2 4 6 8 10 9 7 5 3 1

© 1983 Helen Oxenbury

This book has been typeset in Goudy

Printed in Hong Kong

British Library Cataloguing in Publication Data:
a catalogue record for this book
is available from the British Library

ISBN 0-7445-8183-4

'How can Daddy drive properly
with all that noise going on?' Mum said.

I went with Dad to pay for the petrol.
'Can't I just have some little sweets?' I said.

At lunchtime we went to a cafe.
I only wanted ice cream.

'Just have a little sleep now,' Mum said.
'We won't be home till late.'
'I want to go to the lavatory,' I said.

'I think it's going to rain,' Mum said.
'My tummy hurts, I feel sick,' I said.
'Quick! Stop!' Mum shouted.

We cleaned up the car.
Then it wouldn't start again.
Dad tried and tried, but it was no good.
'I'll have to call a garage for help,' he said.

The truck towed us home.
'We've just had a really great time,'
I told my friends.

For Barnaby

First published 1983 by Walker Books Ltd
87 Vauxhall Walk, London SE11 5HJ

This edition published 2001

2 4 6 8 10 9 7 5 3 1

© 1983 Helen Oxenbury

This book has been typeset in Goudy

Printed in Hong Kong

British Library Cataloguing in Publication Data:
a catalogue record for this book
is available from the British Library

ISBN 0-7445-8178-8